The Girl from America

Ephantus Mwenda

Virtue Book Publishers
Your choice Creative & Publishing Partner

The Girl from America

ISBN: 978-9966-7275-5-8
© Ephantus Mwenda

PO. Box 297-60100
Cell: +254-728-638-801
Embu-Kenya.
Email: mwendanjagi@rocketmail.com
mtkenyaroyalarts@gmail.com

Published by
Virtue Holdings Limited
PO. Box 15417-00100-
Cell: 254-724-529-850

Nairobi-Kenya.
info@virtuebookpublishers.org
www.virtueboopublishers.org

First published in 2016

DEDICATION

To all people who love reading and who find inspiration in my books.

ACKNOWLEDGMENTS

I would like to take this golden opportunity to thank my family for their help in course of writing this book.

Special thanks to the one, Joy Kakelo for the cover photo and Joseph Njagi Kithinji for the final evaluation of this book. Also, I wish to thank my publishers, Virtue Books, for their help since I begun publishing with them in 2011.

I further wish to thank Mr. Khainga O'Okwemba, the host of the premier literature programme on Kenya Broadcasting Corporation- The Books Café, the President of PEN Kenya Centre and a former columnist with The Star newspaper. More thanks to EKITABU LLC Philadelphia USA, one of my books' distributors worldwide.

I finally thank all the authors across the world and especially fiction writers because their work has been my greatest motivation in my writing career.

Special thanks to you for buying this book and also to all my fans across the world.

CONTENTS

CHAPTER 1

Max was sound asleep when his phone began ringing. It rang for several minutes but he seemed to be enjoying something better. He made different kinds of movement, tried to tear blankets, screamed, and roared like a lion. He was dreaming again.

However, this time it was not a question of Vietnam military mission. It was a mission in Southern Sudan. His machine gun hung on his back. He was done with snipes. It was time for a combat mission. This was exactly what he enjoyed most while in a stiff mission. He clenched his fists and moved towards the enemy in a tactful manner. Little did he know, it was a vampire.

"Here we go!" he cried attacking his opponent. It was at this time he jumped out of his bed. Sweat was all over his body. The phone began ringing again. He took a face towel and dried the sweat on his face and hands.

"It can't be. I over slept!" he screamed his hands trembling. It was already 6.30am. As Max held the receiver, he broke into a smile. It was Michelle Catalane - a flying doctor from America, his girlfriend.

"Hello darling, how are you?'' he called.

"I am fine dear. What of you?'' Michelle

replied from the other end. As the conversation between the two lovers went on, Max moved from one point to another in the room, gathering personal effects. His girlfriend had just arrived at Jomo Kenyatta International Airport (JKIA) and he opted to rush there to get her by the next one hour. Max was an ex military captain. He had resigned the previous year aged twenty nine. Though it was a sad moment for him and his colleagues, there was no alternative. This had happened during a deadly peace keeping mission in a neighboring country.

Max's commanding officer had ordered him to carry out the mission with twenty six soldiers including two lieutenants. Max enjoyed such missions and that what gave him a chance to be ranked captain at an age of twenty three years. He had joined military at an innocent age of eighteen immediately after his high school studies.

Max was the last born in a family of three and the only boy. His two sisters were pursuing degree courses in a local university. The eldest of the two, Eunice, was doing a degree course in Actuarial Science. She was at her final year. The younger sister was pursuing one in Economics; she was in her first year at the time he joined the military. Max was the only person in the family who always developed a fever whenever he saw

huge volumes of books.

"I hate cramming for examinations and at the end of it all I always score below average. I wish to engage myself in a tangible thing, military or something of the kind. I dream seeing myself ranked as a commando in the military," he used to tell everyone in the family. No one dared object his ideas, especially his mother. She knew her son very well and deep down knew that her son would make an excellent military officer. His father too was willing to support his only son in whatever conceivable and sensible decision he was to make about his career.

Military is not an awe career at all. His two uncles are doing well there. I remember they used to argue the same," his father kept saying. Therefore, it was not hard for Max to join the military after his high school studies. He had everyone's support.

* * *

As he entered the bathroom, he remembered how he met with Michelle Catalane.

It was five years before his resignation from the military. At that time, was at the border with his fellow soldiers guarding the refugees who had run for their lives from West Africa. Various organizations across the world had come to offer their help in food, clothes, medical

services and other amenities to the refugees. Amur Health Organization from America was among them. They came there specifically to administer medical services. Among the employees of that company was a gorgeous young doctor named Michelle Catalane. On the other hand, Captain Max was in charge of every activity that went on in the refugee camp at the border.

When Michelle and her medical team arrived, Max welcomed them and showed them a proper location to camp. He remembered how he helped them erect their tents despite having men in their team who could have done that. But the truth was- he had seen a diamond.

After instructing the military clerk to liaise with the person in charge from Michelle`s team for any help they needed, he headed straight for this American diamond.

Michelle watched him approaching. Her tremendous figure sat well on her curvilinear waist. Her sparkling eyebrows blinked slightly as she gazed at him increasing his pace towards her. Her delicate ears matching a dainty rose listened at his footsteps. A saccharine heart shaped lips broke into a glorious smile revealing a shiny halo-white teeth. Her ebony-black hair flowed gently over her shoulders and she wholly reflected a winning-joyous personality. At last, Max stood before her.

"I am Captain Maxwell, the military commanding officer in this camp," he said stretching his hand for a hand shake.

"I am Doctor Michelle Catalane. Nice to meet you Captain Maxwell," she answered with a smile that left the soldier confused. He had never been in such a situation before during his military career. He was not sure of what to do or say next. For seconds, he just stood there smiling back.

"I believe we will be meeting regularly Captain Max," Michelle said at last.

"Yeah," Max answered but one could tell that he was absent minded. Michelle appeared to understand the effect she had caused on him.

She swiftly excused herself and joined her fellow medical practitioners. Max turned and watched her as she moved from one point to another. She appeared smart in that white coat and a pair of stethoscope hanging over her neck.

"I swear she is cute!" he said aloud walking back to his colleagues.

"Is everything alright sir?" Lieutenant Mark asked.

"Oh..., yes lieutenant," Max answered smiling. Mark was his best friend in the military. They had trained together and were glad to be

grouped together almost in all missions. The Major seemed to understand it. All the same, they used to conduct their missions so well and the Major was always happy with their results.

"Sir, she looks magnificent. I saw how you stared at each other. It seemed like love at first sight," Mark said.

"Forget it Mark," Max replied hilariously.

"I bet I'm right," Mark said.

"I believe that she is good. One can speak of that. However, time will tell," Max answered.

"That's exactly what I wanted to hear, it's a golden chance. Use it wisely sir," Mark said. At this, Max smiled broadly.

"You are right Mark. It is a golden chance!" he said getting into his tent. The soldier guarding the tent heard it and smiled too.

* * *

Since that day hence forth, Max had a new role at the camp, a role of a man in love. He visited Michelle's work place as many times as he could but he never at a single second neglected his duties as the officer in charge of the camp. He just wanted to watch Michelle handling the patients with minor injuries. Those with major injuries were referred to the National Hospital and transported by military helicopters. On the other hand, Michelle as well enjoyed his

presence and the sense of security he offered. It was not safe in the camp but with Captain Max around, she felt like she was in a safe house somewhere in New York City.

On the other side, Max enjoyed seeing how Michelle handled patients with care. He longed for a minor injury if only he could end up in her arms. He longed to hold those tender film star hands. He longed to feel them attending to an injury on his body if he had any.

Sometimes, when there were no patients to be attended, they held long conversations and that brought them closer to each other. They took long drives around the huge camp and no doubt; one could clearly tell that something right was going on between the two. As time went, they became fonder of each other. People like Mark couldn't help his joy. He was already convinced that this American diamond was a perfect match for the Captain.

"Our Captain and Michelle have become so intimate," Mark said to his fellow soldiers.

It was seven months since the lovebirds had met. The attacks had ceased in West Africa and most of the refugees had set their minds to return to their countries. The security at the camp was guaranteed and several soldiers were sent back to their barracks. At that time, Max decided that it was time to show his girlfriend a little of his country. Michelle spoke with her boss- one in charge of their medical team and she was delighted when she was granted a seven day leave.

With the help of a military helicopter, Max and his girlfriend found their way to Kenya. The captain had a house at the outskirts of Nairobi city. This would hold them away from everything else and grant them an ample time to meditate on what they felt for each other.

On getting to the city centre, Max hired a private car after doing a week's shopping. The city appeared great and serene for Michelle. The air was more fresh compared to the camp and she felt peaceful. The driver drove them towards Thika highway and stopped somewhere in Ruiru- an estate where Max lived. The driver assisted them by carrying their luggage and some other items. Max paid him and he left.

"What did you call this place?'' Michelle asked as soon as the driver left.

"Ruiru,'' Max answered with laugher slight laughter. Michelle tried to pronounce the name several times replacing the `r' with `l'. It was a great fun for them.

Max moved around the house checking whether everything was in order for his girlfriend. The security guard at the gate was performing well as was expected. Everything was

fine and Max had no reason to question anything. Since the time he took charge at the camp, he had only visited his house twice. That marked a total of six days during the eleven months he had been at the border.

This time he had a chance to bring a friend around. Before he began his house chores, he showed Michelle the shower upstairs. His house had two bedrooms and that was fine with him. During the time they had been together at the camp, they had not crossed the boundaries in their relationship and- he wanted things to remain that way. Michelle was a wonderful lady and his first girlfriend since leaving the military college several years back.

As Michelle showered, he ensured that her room was in perfect shape. Once she was done with bathing, she was overwhelmed to see how Max had made everything look so colourful in there. Max was the man she had longed for. He had extra-ordinary characteristics. She now understood why he was promoted to the rank of a captain at such an early age. The Major and other top officials must have seen those extra-ordinary traits in him.

"Thank you so much Captain for everything," she said smiling.

"You're welcome my dear angel. Feel free to ask for anything you need," Max answered

feeling uneasy. Michelle could not forget the title 'Captain' even after Max insisted that she was free to call him Maxwell or Max as she preferred. He stood there smiling at Michelle who was swiftly scanning the room. At last, one could tell that she liked everything in it, including the man before her.

"Great Captain!" she said hugging him, "I'm feeling hungry. Is there a kitchen in this house?" she asked teasingly amid laughter.

"We can check on the blue prints," Max answered in laughter. They left the room, moved past the living room and got in the kitchen.

"I bet I can devour a whole elephant. The lunch we had at the city centre is far gone," Max said as he poured a drink into the glasses. After a toast, they gulped their drinks in silence.

"I need another one here," Michelle said in laughter handing him her glass.

"At your service my dear," Max said. He poured the drink in their glasses again. However, this time none was in a hurry to take it. They seemed satisfied. They began preparing something to eat in great joy. Each of them could cook and they ended up with a great recipe.

That week marked a significant milestone in their life. They were totally assured that they were in love and nothing could alter that-it was a magical moment for them.

"You are amazing darling," Mitchell gushed at the end of it all.

CHAPTER 2

Max was ready to leave for the airport. He wore his military gears- a t-shirt, a short and a pair of martial black leather shoes. He took a small bag and put everything he needed for the short journey. He always behaved like a soldier.

It's a career he loved and missed, but fate had determined otherwise. The reason for his resignation was his health status. The doctor had ordered him to stay away from his job after a botched mission to rescue four media agents, and two school kids who had been kidnapped by an opposition military group in a neighbouring country.

The leader of the military group was under the influence of a court that trained young persons' to oppose the government and overthrow the president. However, through the help of the United Nations, they were stopped.

Max and his team were sent there. He personally rescued the two kids from the den of lions and that's when a bullet from his enemy pierced his skull leaving behind a severe injury. However, they successfully completed the mission. Max was transported to the country by an emergency military helicopter and was taken to the National Hospital where he was placed under intensive care unit for a period of six days.

"The bullet didn't cause much damage on his skull," the doctors assured everyone, "He is out of danger," he added.

However, since then, Max found himself in a trying period. The scenario kept tormenting his mind and heart. He sometimes behaved like a person in a battle field whenever he saw his fellow soldiers in their troops. He couldn't even stand an action movie and thus, his family and the doctors suggested that it would be safe for him to stay away from his work. He personally opted to resign and promised to be of help whenever a need arose.

"I think am better now. I rarely see myself in the battle field. However, I have made up my mind to do something else," he told Mark who had paid him a visit several weeks later. After his resignation, Mark was appointed as the new captain. At the time, Max was overjoyed and happy for his friend and he felt at peace.

"I can't regret my decision. A hero has already taken my position. It feels so wonderful," he confessed to Mark.

"I'm humbled captain to have you as my friend and mentor," Mark said proudly saluting at Max.

* * *

Max called Michelle to announce that he was on his way. He started his jeep and in a few

seconds, he was on the highway towards the city centre. However, before long, he realized that there was such a traffic jam than he had ever witnessed before. Ahead of him in the highway were hundreds of vehicles of all kinds. He tried to enquire what was going on from several drivers and he learnt that there was a dreadful riot going on three hundred meters ahead.

"Why are people rioting?" he asked a lorry driver.

"You should know better. You seem to be one of them sir," the driver answered and Max cursed secretly for the driver's observation.

"I`m retired sir," he said at last.

"You must be kidding! You are barely thirty five and you talk about retiring? Tell it to the marines," the driver answered puffing a cigarette.

"It's alright sir. Let forget about it. Just tell me what is happening. I've just arrived. I wasn't around here," he tried another line of conversation.

"Hey! Soldier, you should have said that. They are complaining about massive accidents on this highway. They want the roads authority to do something about it," the driver answered puffing the smoke through his truck's window.

"This is bad. I will be late if something is not done," Max said breathing out hard.

"Don't worry soldier. Your colleagues are doing their best. I must say you are a good people. We can't do without you guys!'' the driver said smiling broadly. Max's mind was long gone. The driver was speaking to a log. He was thinking of a way he would get to the airport before an hour was over. 'This is really bad!' he thought.

"Soldier, right now I feel like a minister himself. A handsome soldier guarding me is a guaranteed maximum security!'' the driver shouted in laughter. Max never said a word. He walked back to his jeep and took his small bag and run towards the huge crowd.

"That's great of you soldier! Help your fellow soldiers to clear the way! I must get this old bird to the company on time before the boss gets angry!'' the driver shouted. Within five minutes, Max had come to the scene. The immense crowd had used all sorts of things to set a road block on the highway: large stones, burning tires and tins. The police officers began to fire shots in the air and the crowd began to scream even louder while running helter skelter. Some threw stones at the officers and the situation deteriorated rapidly. Another team of police began firing tear gas to the crowd. The crowd began scattering rapidly clearing from the highway.

The Girl From America

Max reached for his small bag and got out a bottle of water and a handkerchief. He soaked the handkerchief in water and covered his nose. He reached for his military goggles and wore them before he became a victim of the tear gas. He ensured that his little bag was safe as he began running away from the wild crowd. In the process of it, he noticed a little girl lying on the road screaming helplessly.

The girl appeared injured and was nose bleeding. Max gathered his strength and pushed his way through the mob. A life was at risk and he was to do his best to save the girl.

At last, he reached for her and took her in his arms. The angry crowd was now throwing more and more stones without caring the damage they caused. The situation was awful.

"We must get out of here quickly or else these fools will kill us," Max told the girl. Luckily, he found his way out of the crowd and began running towards his jeep. He also realized that any vehicle near the crowd had no glass on it. He wondered about the state of their owners.

Returning to the jeep, he placed the girl on the front seat. He then untied the handkerchief above his nose and took off his goggles. He then searched through his tiny bag and reached for the bottle of water and another handkerchief. All this time, the lorry driver who was keenly looking at him gaped. Max gave the water to the little girl who was chocking from the gas. He also washed her face and dried the blood on her nostrils and on the slight bruises on her face.

"Don't worry my little angel. You will be well," Max told the little girl smiling and she smiled back.

"Good work soldier. I knew you would do something great!" the truck driver said applauding.

"Great compliment. But it's nothing big, thank you!" Max replied.

"You see soldier, I haven't moved an inch. I wanted to keep an eye on your little plane," the driver said again pointing at Max's jeep.

"Thank you so much," Max said.

Max went ahead to attend to the girl until he was sure that she was well. After the first aid, he decided to ask her some questions that would help him to decide on the next move. Nevertheless, before that, he stepped out of the jeep, and stood on its bonnet and glanced at the crowd. The firing had ceased, but the tear gas was still flying in the air like grenades.

"I must get this kid to the hospital for a check up. I am not certain she is ok," he said to the driver.

"That's very kind of you soldier. As for me, I know that my boss is now angry enough to fire me," the driver said in low spirit.

"Don't worry. He will understand. The media is here and I am sure he is now aware of why you are late," Max told him.

"He won't understand. He is a hard nut to crack. He expects someone to find his way in such a situation. Even if it means flying," the driver answered in slight laughter.

"I feel sorry for you. But don't lose your faith. Stick to it and it might change things," Max said stepping down from the bonnet.

"You are right soldier. We can now be able to move an inch. My speedometer is already reading five," the driver answered in delight. Max got back to his jeep and drove slowly as he spoke with the driver. In a short while, it was impossible for them to see each other as Max was concentrating on making his way past the other vehicles.

"What is your name pretty angel?" Max asked her.

"My name is Sophie Hassan," she answered

"Wow! That's a lovely name. Where are your parents Sophie?"

"I live with my mother. We were en route to school when we met the bad people. We then

lost sight of each other when the police started throwing the smoky bombs,'' she explained. Max almost broke into laughter but realized that, it was not the right moment to do so. He smiled as he drove. They were already in the city centre. He made his way towards the university way and went past central park towards Ngong road

"That sounds bad. But don't worry my pretty Sophie. I must take you to the hospital for a medical examination. Okay?''

"It's alright. What's your name?''

"Oh… I'm Maxwell. But most people including my mother calls me Max,'' he said in a childish voice and they both broke into laughter.

"How old are you Sophie?''

"Nine years old." She answered.

The conversation continued and Sophie answered all the questions leaving Max amazed by her intelligence. Now, he had all the information he needed. He knew that he would get Sophie to her mother soon. He also learnt from the questioning that Sophie's mother was a teacher in the same school she was schooling. He was glad to learn that he would trace her mother in no time.

"We have arrived. This is the National Hospital. Have you ever been here before?'' Max asked.

"No," Sophie answered slightly afraid. Max realized it.

"My pretty Sophie, don't be afraid," he said driving towards the reserved parking at the hospital.

"Max, I am afraid of the injection!" she said horrified.

"Oh...that. Don't worry my dear. You don't need one," he said smiling while parking the jeep.

"Are you sure?" she asked brightening up.

"Yeah," he answered getting out of the jeep. They both walked to the reception hall. Sophie held Max`s hand firmly. On getting there, Max was aghast, the queue was too long and he also realized that the crowd he saw outside the reception hall was part of the queue.

"We must do something my dear," he said carrying her on his arms. Although she was nine years old, she appeared somewhat bigger than her age reflected. Max pushed his way towards the reception table and stood before two nurses.

"What the hell do you think you are doing going past everyone!" A man bellowed behind him but he took no notice. What mattered was to get Sophie examined as soon as possible. He was still afraid that the girl might have internal injuries that she might not be aware of it. 'She is too young to differentiate external and internal injuries,' Max had thought. One nurse stared at his clothes and asked whether he was a military.

"I am an ex-military captain. I like the outfit because it reminds me a lot of my former work,'' Max told her loudly.

"I am so sorry Captain. I should not have shouted at you!'' The man who had yelled at him avowed. Everyone glanced at him and even those in great pain tried to force a smile. Max didn't look at him like everyone else did. He was busy giving the details of the riot and how he found Sophie in the middle of it. Everything was recorded in a computer and the nurse told him to go to the room adjacent to the second reception hall: room number 12.

"It's the medical examination area Captain,'' the nurse added.

"Thank you so much,'' he said to the nurses and also repeated the same to everyone behind him in the queue and left for the room number 12.

"I never thought that he is such a disciplined soldier!'' The same man shouted and this time everyone laughed aloud.

* * *

Max found himself in another spacious reception hall. On his left stood a door with a placard reading, 'Medical Examination R.No.12. ' He wondered whether to go in instantly or to wait like everyone else on the benches. Before he could decide, one of the nurses from the first reception hall came and led him into the room. She mentioned the name of the little girl to her colleagues and one of them turned to the computer. Max realized that every data in the entire hospital was digitized. He remembered the head of the state saying about it a month earlier but he not thought everything would be implemented so fast.

'This is really the digital age,' he contemplated.

The nurses asked him to leave and wait for the results. Sophie had already been taken to another room for further medical examination. Max went out of the room and sat on the bench in the reception hall. He realized that everyone was looking at him keenly and he felt bemused. Then, they turned their eyes to the large T.V. screen on one side of the reception hall. It's at that point when Max realized that his face was on T.V and Sophie in his arms on the news bulletin.

It was already 9.00am. He didn't realize how that happened. He never saw a single media

agent as he struggled to save Sophie. However, he knew that he was too busy to think of the media at the time: a chance for everyone for himself. He looked at everyone in the hall and smiled broadly.

"That was a good job captain," Max heard the voice and remembered it was from the same man who had shouted at him at the other reception hall. He turned and their eyes met. The man smiled and he smiled back. The nurse called his name and he went in. Sophie was calmly seated on the chair and she smiled at Max and he smiled back. One of the nurses noticed it and smiled too.

"Here is the results sir." A printed paper was handed over to him by one of the nurses.

"As you can see, we have examined her rigorously and she is in good health," the nurse concluded.

"Thank you so much. These are excellent news. Can we leave now?" Max asked.

"Yes, but you will pass through the dressing room as indicated on her results for the sake of the slight bruises on her left cheek," the nurse replied.

"I will do that. Thank you," he said picking up Sophie. The doctor emerged from the examination room and told the nurses to call in another patient. In less than twenty minutes,

Max and Sophie were already in the jeep ready to leave. For the first time since they met, Max realized that Sophie was on her school uniform. He was greatly astonished by the comings and goings of the day that had left him so confused.

"From here, we will rush at the airport, pick someone and drive to your School. Your mother must be worried about your whereabouts. She might have reported it to the police."

"My mother is a wonderful person. She will be happy and thankful for helping me," Sophie said taking her soda. Max had bought the drinks at one of the kiosks near the hospital on their way out.

"That is wonderful. Let's get moving," Max said accelerating the vehicle. He sped down the Ngong road towards the city centre. In no time, he found himself on Mombasa road. He had avoided the Jogoo road because it was known to have massive traffic jams during morning rush hour. Mombasa road appeared clear and vehicle moved smoothly. He knew by the next twenty minutes, they would be at Jomo Kenyatta International Airport.

CHAPTER 3

Max arrived at the airport's arrival department and drove towards the reserved parking. He took Sophie in his arms and headed towards the airport hotel. He knew that Michelle was worried for taking so long. Since their first meeting; Michelle had been visiting every year for the last four years. Whenever she came to the country, she always waited for Max in the airport hotel and twice- she found him waiting for her.

As soon as Max entered the hotel, their eyes met. Michelle was occupying a table set in the middle of the hotel. Max heartbeat increased as he moved in long strides. Sophie appeared to understand what was coming and she instinctively released Max's left hand as they approached Michelle who had already stood up smiling winsomely; her hands wide open for her long awaited boyfriend. In no time, they dissolved in each other's arms.

"I'm sorry for coming late darling. I swear I have missed you dearly,'' Max said after a long hugging.

"Don't worry my love. I already know what had kept you that long,'' Michelle said smiling. Max got to quick thinking and his eyes landed on a large slim Samsung T.V screen fixed on one of the hotel walls.

"You want to say you saw me on the news bulletin?"

"Yeah, with this lovely angel," Michelle said bending to hug Sophie. Max was confused for a moment. But on recovery, he introduced Sophie to Michelle and vice versa. He also narrated in short what had happened and Michelle was overwhelmed by his act of mercy.

"Even if I could not have seen you on the bulletin, I could have guessed you were somewhere doing a good thing honey!" Michelle said kissing his right cheek.

"I can't desire for more darling. All what I need in this world is you- Michelle Catalane!" Max declared and after some minutes of, they were in the jeep heading to his place.

* * *

Max`s mind was in a hot game. He wanted to arrive home quickly and before everything else, head to Sophie's school or home depending with the circumstances. Michelle was willing to assist him until the little girl was back to her parents.

So, on arrival, they wasted no time. They took the luggage to the house and waited for Michelle to take a quick shower to aid her ease the journey's lethargy. She had already taken her breakfast at the airport hotel and as soon as she

was through, they headed to Kasarani, a few kilometres from Ruiru, where Sophie and her mother lived. By then, it was some minutes to 12:00 noon. Sophie knew their place so well and it took them a little time to get there.

"It seems there is no one in,'' Max said after glancing the building. Sophie called out aloud but there was no answer. They moved around the building and there was no sign of a human being.

"Sophie, do you have a house help?'' Max asked.

"No, I live with my mother,'' she answered.

"My dear, time is not on our side, I think we should drive to the school,'' Michelle said at last.

"That a brilliant idea. Her mother teaches there too,'' Max answered smiling.

"I forgot to tell you Max. My mom is a Mathematics teacher,'' Sophie said hysterically.

"Wow! That amazing, let go!'' Michelle shouted reaching for her. They went to the jeep playfully.

* * *

It didn't take him long to arrive at Ruiru Star Academy: where Sophie schooled. After parking the jeep, Max asked Sophie and Michelle

to wait there as he went to see the head master. On getting inside the head teacher's office, he met the secretary who was busy typing a report.

"Good afternoon," Max greeted her.

"Good afternoon to you," the secretary answered raising her head to look at the person in front of her. From her sitting position, she seemed amazed by Max's height, his robustly built body and the natural smile on his face.

'He is so handsome,' the secretary thought for a moment.

"Kindly take a seat sir," the secretary said pointing to the chair next to her desk. Max obeyed and sat.

"My name is Maxwell. However, everyone prefers to call me Max and I am here to see the head teacher," he said.

"Alright Mr. Maxwell, I am Cate," she said and smiled at him, "You are lucky to find him. He will be leaving in a few minutes for an important meeting. Are you in the military?" she asked with curiosity registering on her face.

"Oh..., that?" Max was amused for a moment. He never expected such a question. He glanced at his clothes and looked up at Cate smiling.

"I was in the military but resigned last year," he answered flatly. He prayed secretly that the conversation wouldn't go any further. He

wanted to see the head teacher and end his business at the school as fast as he could.

"That sounds fascinating Mr. Max. I wish the head teacher was not in a hurry. You could have told me more about your experience in the military," Cate said, she noticed the scar on Max's head. She seemed to understand that every minute spent then was so important to Max. She stood up and walked towards the head teacher's door. She knocked and went in. After a minute, she emerged smiling and told Max that the head teacher was waiting for him.

"Thank you so much Cate," he said walking inside the head teacher's office.

"At your service Mr. Max," Cate answered resuming her seat. Max went inside the office and after exchanging greetings with the head teacher, he began his story about Sophie. The head teacher was all ears and he never interrupted him once. He knew Sophie so well because her mother was part of the staff. They had not got any report on the whereabouts of Miss Sarah Hassan, the Mathematics teacher.

"I fear she might have fallen victim of the rioting," the head teacher said at last. He seemed worried about the situation.

"I am afraid that might set hurdles for Sophie," Max said.

"Wait a minute Mr. Max," the head teacher said lifting the receiver of his office phone. He dialled a number and waited. He then began a conversation which, from the expressions on his face didn't bear positive results. He went on dialling more numbers for a period of fifteen minutes and at last he appeared exhausted and worried.

"I have tried all the persons I know including his contact people and no one is aware of her whereabouts. I think we should report the matter to the police," the head teacher said.

"That's a good idea. But I think it's too early to start jumping into conclusions. The rioting took place a few hours ago and it might be hard to gather any valuable information about the victims now," Max said, "However, I have a friend of mine, the Secretary General of Riverwood T.V. I might make my first step there and see whether they have anything helpful from the riot.

After that, I can consider reporting her disappearance to the police at the Central Police Station. By doing that, it means if Miss Hassan is somewhere out there looking for her daughter, the T.V will play it role by letting her know that where her daughter is," Max concluded.

"I agree with you. She might have reported to the police too about the loss of her

daughter during the rioting. So by going there, that might as well save the situation,'' the head teacher said.

"One more thing Mr. headmaster, what if the worst has happened and we find out that your teacher was among the severely injured persons during the rioting?'' Max asked.

"I think if that happen Mr. Max, we will handle the situation just like it will be. Don't worry; I and my institution will be wide awake in case you need urgent assistance. I have a meeting in town and we can walk out together as I speak with Sophie,'' the head teacher concluded.

The two men exited the office and walked past Cate. Max waved and smiled to her, and she waved and smiled back. Since Max entered the head teacher's office, Cate had done nothing. The piece of work she was typing before Max arrived still stared at her on the computer. She was in deep thoughts.She had never seen such a handsome man before. The situation and thoughts shocked her as well.

"What's wrong with me?'' she asked staring hard on the computer. She wondered where Max lived and whether he was married. She tried to remember whether she had seen a wedding ring on his finger but couldn't remember it vividly.

"But nowadays weddings do not fall within much value. He might have married in the traditional way. Oh no! He might be single! He must, because of me!" she screamed glaring at the computer. She wondered why Max was there and swore to enquire about it from the head teacher the following day.

* * *

Max drove fast past the city centre towards Prestige Plaza, where Riverwood T.V was located. He knew that he was up to the right time and, there was a chance of meeting the Secretary General at the T.V station. He had not called him to confirm that but he was sure to find him there. Since they left Sophie's school, he kept making fleeting looks at Michelle and Sophie at the back seat of the jeep and realized they had grown fond of each other in such a brief moment. They played and poked one another amidst great laughter.

Max slowed down and turned to the left, towards the main gate of the Riverwood T.V Broadcasting Centre. The security guards at the gate knew him so well and waved at him as they opened the heavy gate. He drove in slowly and parked his jeep at the little space left in the parking area.

"Now we get moving," he announced to them getting out of the jeep. Michelle and Sophie followed staring at the lovely building.

"It's nicely built. I just like it!" Michelle declared.

"It's one of the best buildings in the city," Max replied as they entered the reception room. He enquired whether the Secretary General was in and he was told that he hasn't gone out since morning. Max thanked her and together with his team, they headed to the lift which took them to the eighth floor. He was familiar with the place and thus he didn't have to enquire where to find his friend Steve, the Secretary General.

"His office is room number three," he told Michelle. They moved towards the room and he stopped to knock the door. He heard Steve`s voice urging whoever was out there to get in. Max smiled at Michelle and Sophie.

"It will be a great chance for both of you to meet the man and the best T.V broadcaster in Africa," Max announced to them as they went inside. Steve raised his head and burst out with a shout of joy.

"It's such a long time man. Where have you been in this world?" he asked standing to shake their hands.

"I have been in the country my friend. Just doing business here and there,'' Max answered shaking his friend's hand dynamically.

"That's fantastic my friend. It seems you have great ladies here,'' Steve said shaking hands with Michelle and Sophie.

"She is Michelle-my girlfriend. I remember telling you about her,'' Max said.

"Yes, I do recall that so well. Has she been here for long?''

"She arrived this morning; next to her is a great friend of us: princes Sophie!'' Max announced.

"Wonderful to meet such gorgeous ladies,'' he answered directing them to a large black leather couch on one side of his office. He also enquired on the kind of drinks they wanted and went for them at the fridge on one corner of the life-size office.

"You should have announced her arrival. Even if it meant a five seconds phone call,'' Steve said to Max.

"I'm sorry Steve, I had such a complicated busy morning.''

"Even so, I hope everything is okay brother,'' Steve said glancing at the three of them in turn. He noticed the little bruises on Sophie's cheeks.

"What happened to her?'' he asked sitting on another little couch next to them.

"Allow me to finish my drink and I will tell you all about it,'' Max said teasingly.

"Alright, but if I had known about your visit, I could have organized a thirty minutes live interview. I believe you guys can't miss a message for the nation and especially her,'' Steve said pointing at Michelle, "Her experience as a flying medical practitioner has a lot for the world to hear and determine,'' he added looking straight at Michelle's eyes.

"You are right. It could be such a great pleasure to me and the world,'' Michelle said.

"She will be here for three months. You can organize an interview for her anytime you want,'' Max said warmly. He seemed to like the idea.

"I will. In fact, I'll start working on it instantly!'' Steve said amid joy. They sipped their drinks for a moment without saying a word. Then, Steve broke the silence.

"I know that you're quite a busy person, coming here at this time of the day means a great deal to me. What do I owe the visit brother?''

At this point, Max understood it was time for business. He introduced Sophie to Steve more widely and explained the events of the day since he left his house early in the morning.

Steve remained attentive to every piece of information that Max narrated to him. His station was widely broadcasting about that riot and its effects and here was another burning bit of it. As soon as Max concluded, Steve smiled and expressed his gratitude for coming. He explained how significant the information was and that he had already allocated a team of professionals to work on the riot story to the end.

He confessed that Sophie's case was another hot piece of it and that his company would make every reasonable effort to reunite Sophie with her mother. He promised to gather as much information as he could to help the little girl.

"We will also check the police stations, to all the hospitals in the city and I believe at the end of it Sophie will find her mother. We haven't received a death case report as a result of the riot and therefore you should not worry yourselves. Sophie's mother is somewhere in town and our media team will reach her in no time," Steve assured them.

"You have no idea how glad I am to learn that. You are great Steve. I knew right from the beginning that you would help us. Thank you brother," Max said.

"I know you people will make the best from our minute information. I must say I love

that spirit of work,'' Michelle declared. Everyone nodded including the little Sophie.

From there, Max and his team headed to the Central Police Station. He knew that he had done more than enough but it was also very important to report to the police that he was the one hosting Sophie. That could ease the work ahead of them. Also, as an ex-military, he knew it was not safe to have a lost kid without notifying the police about it.

Therefore, on getting there, a statement was drawn up and the Base Commanding Officer thanked him for helping the child. He also asked for permission to keep her at his place and was granted the request. After ensuring that everything was in order, they left knowing very soon they will hear from the police, Riverwood T.V or Ruiru Star Academy about Sophie's mother.

CHAPTER 4

It was three days gone. Max patiently waited for any information concerning the whereabouts of Sophie's mother. However, he tried his best to conceal his fears from Michelle and Sophie. He had driven to Sophie's home a day before to enquire from the neighbours whether they had any information on the subject of Sophie's mother but not a single one of them was of help. Some neighbours were shocked when they learnt that their neighbour was one of those caught up in the dangerous riot.

"We are really sorry sir. But as soon as I hear anything I will let you know instantly," a neighbourhood woman assured him. Max thanked her and left. He had made several calls to Steve and he had no new information.

Now, he was in a small flower garden behind his house thoughtfully. Michelle was busy in the house and Sophie was already at school. Max and Michelle had bought her everything she needed for her studies because they didn't know when Miss Hassan would show up. Max was glad to see Sophie resuming her studies. Michelle was in the same mood too. Both appeared to love this young girl. She had become one of them in such a short time.

"Darling Max, you have a phone call," Michelle announced walking towards him with a ringing mobile phone in her hands. Max stood up and moved rapidly towards her. He desperately desired some good news from whatever source.

"Thank you dear," he said taking the phone from her.

"Hello," he said.

"Hello to you. I'm sure this is Maxwell," the voice from the other end said.

"May I know who I'm talking to please?" Max asked. The person on the line identified himself as the Base Commanding Officer from the Central Police. He said that they have already received a positive report in regard to Miss Hassan`s whereabouts.

"Where is she?" Max could not resist himself from asking.

"She is admitted at Kikuyu General Hospital since the day of the riot," the officer said. After the conversation, Max could not wait. He told Michelle all about it and they hurriedly prepared to leave to see her.

* * *

They arrived at the hospital an hour later. After parking the jeep, they hurried to the reception and after introducing themselves, enquired to see Miss Hassan. The nurse at the

reception required them to wait as she confirmed the details of the patient. They hopefully sat on a bench in the reception hall and waited.

"Mr. Maxwell!" the nurse called a few minutes later. Max and Michelle stood and walked to the reception table. The nurse explained to them that they could only be allowed to see her for a few minutes. She explained that she was in a critical situation after the attack during the rioting.

"She was brought here by the Red Cross rescue team," the nurse said.

"Good heavens! It sounds awful," Michelle interjected.

"The doctors have done their best and her life is out of danger. It appeared that someone had mercilessly thrown a stone or something of the kind that almost crushed her skull," the nurse explained.

Max listened to all this speechless. He remembered what had happened to him during that rescue mission and how a bullet missed the centre of his cranium. He shivered and glared at the floor. Michelle was in a good position to handle the report because she was used to handling patients in such critical conditions. She looked at Max and she could tell why he was so quite. She personally attended to him when she received a call telling of the bad news.

"It's okay darling. That's long gone. Let's focus on what's at hand now," Michelle said rubbing his back.

Max seemed to recover amazingly. He was in the right hands and that's what encouraged him. He turned and looked at Michelle straight in her eyes. They both smiled at each other and hugged. The nurse from the other side seemed to miss every single moment of it.

'What a wonderful couple!' she pondered.

Without wasting much time, the nurse led them to the ward where Miss Hassan was admitted. On getting there, Michelle understood by the look of her eyes how she was fairing.

"We took her out of intensive care unit six hours ago." Another nurse who was watching over her said. The nurse who had accompanied them from the reception left.

"That's good news," Michelle said. Max nodded trying to force a smile.

Miss Hassan opened her eyes and looked at the visitors. She lay on a bed with an inhaler above her nose.

"Everyone here was shocked to see how quickly she made it out of I.C.U. It has never happened before with patients in such a

condition. We thought that a powerful spirit was in control of her healing," the nurse said.

"It's the thought of her daughter," Max interpolated.

"Does she have a kid?" the nurse asked a little shocked.

"Yes, a very beautiful angel. She resembles her mother ninety nine percent," Michelle said warmly. Miss Hassan appeared to get what they were saying. She moved her head as if about to say something. Her lips moved a little too.

"She seems to hear us very well. It`s like she wants to say something," Max observed.

"That`s true. But for now we can`t allow anyone to engage her in a conversation, she is too weak and she needs enough rest for quick recovery," the nurse said.

"Yeah, I understand what you are saying. But I know one more thing that will improve her condition," Michelle said and walked close to her bed.

"Miss Hassan. Be at peace. Your daughter is in safe hands. She is staying with us and she has already resumed her studies. We wish you speedy recovery dear sister. We will make arrangements on how we can bring dear Sophie to see you," Michelle said smiling warmly. The nurse and Max smiled too. Miss Hassan tried to

smile and at last she made it. That was a big sign. Michelle bent over her carefully and kissed her brow.

"We will be visiting tomorrow in the morning. I want to find you playing around happily," Max said teasingly. Miss Hassan tried another smile. The nurse seemed to like these visitors. If it was within her power, she could have requested them to tour every ward in the entire hospital and speak a word of hope to every patient.

"I like you guys. I wish I could be seeing you every day at this place," the nurse confessed as she escorted them out of the ward.

Max and Michelle glanced at each other and smiled in bliss. They were happy to hear those compliments. They parted with the nurse promising to be there again the following day. They walked side by side and went to thank the nurse at the reception for everything. After that, they left the place in great joy. At last, they had found Miss Hassan, Sophie's mother. They knew very well that it was great news for Sophie too.

"The little angel will fly in joy on receiving the news," Max said as they drove towards the city centre.

"The little angel deserves our help Max. She is so darling," Michelle stated.

"My dear, you are such an awesome angel too. I can't wish for more. I'm sure that the stars in heaven will unite and form a sign of your name darling," Max said.

"Oh! Like to thank you my dear, you are the best," she answered amid tears of joy.

"You are wrong darling. I don't want to be your best. I want to be your favourite and forget the rest!" Max stated amid laughter.

"I never knew you are such a great poet!" she exclaimed in laughter too.

They drove amid immeasurable joy. On getting to the city centre, they chose to have their lunch there. They searched for a best hotel with reserved parking and settled for their lunch.

"The doctor who operated her seems to be so skilled;" Max began the conversation. They were already through with having their lunch and were now refreshing themselves with some drinks.

"That's how it should be. That's what inspired me to take a career in medicine. I felt obligated to work for the people and my passion has led me to great achievement," Michelle said.

"I am thankful for you dear. God will greatly reward you for your excellent service. I thought you would ask for permission to examine her."

"I could have done so. In fact I felt a strong urge to do so from the moment I stepped in that ward. But all the same, from my experience, I could tell she was doing better. But I can do further examination on her tomorrow."

"That's wonderful darling. I can`t wait to see her home for her daughter," he grinned in delight.

After they were through, they decided to spend some time at the city centre touring a few areas. Michelle seemed to enjoy every single moment of it. She had never been in such joy before in her life. Max felt the same too. Later, they drove to Ruiru Star Academy to pick Sophie. Max found the head teacher and explained everything to him. The head teacher was so blissful and announced that he would visit her the following day. He also promised to offer any assistance needed.

"I'm so glad for your help and service to Sophie too. A bright future waits for you young man!" the head teacher had said. Michelle and Max left the office in great joy. They now understood even better the importance of doing good and being good to others.

"My greatest mission under the sun will be, to do well to others all the days of my life!" Max declared as they drove back to their place.

"Your mission began so long darling. It's only that no one had honestly disclosed it to you like he has done," Michelle said.

CHAPTER 5

Two weeks were already gone when Max received a report from the doctor that Miss Hassan would be discharged the following day.

"At last she has made it!" Max announced happily.

"She is an iron woman. It will be great news for little Sophie," Michelle replied. They began setting everything up because they wanted to host Miss Hassan once she was discharged. Max had set aside a small room for Sophie and exhausted any other space left. He knew very well that he could not ask Sophie's mother to spend the night on a couch and thus something had to be done.

They still occupied separate bedrooms with Michelle and an idea came over him. He decided to ask Michelle to evacuate the room for Sophie's mother but wondered what would follow next. However, he concentrated with the events of the day and waited for the right time to talk to her.

In the evening, he drove to Sophie's school to pick her and also told the head teacher that the doctor had called him during the day and announced that Miss Hassan would be discharged the following day.

"That's good news. We have undergone enough trouble in our school already. I`m glad she has made it," the head teacher said.

"What kind of trouble?" Max asked.

"Don't mind that Mr. Maxwell. What I mean is that Miss Hassan was the only Mathematics teacher in the upper classes. So you can imagine what has been happening here."

"Yeah, I can see your point sir," Max said nodding.

"Some parents have been coming here to complain. They even threatened to transfer their kids if the school was not in a position to employ another teacher. However, I had faith that Miss Hassan would make it on time and save us from the hard situation."

"You are a great man. Taking such a risk is not a joke my friend," Max assured him.

"That's true. But there is another thing about it. Our pupils love Miss Hassan so much that they can't do with another teacher," the head teacher said.

"It happens sometimes, especially when the teacher has a sound and healthy relationship with the pupils. But the truth is, Miss Hassan is a great person!" Max stated.

Later, they made all the necessary arrangements and the head teacher asked three teachers to accompany Max to the hospital the

following day. Sophie was also instructed to stay home the following day but she was never told the reason. The head teacher went for her; in her class and announced so.

Max had requested the head teacher the favour so that he could prepare a nice surprise for her. After taking Sophie home, he went to town to buy everything else they required for their guests and the newly found friend- Sophie's mother. There would be a huge party at his place the following day and he wanted to set everything in order. Back in the house, Michelle and the little Sophie did everything possible to ensure that everything else was in order as Max had hoped.

"Aunt," Sophie called, "what are these decorations for?" Sophie asked Michelle.

"Uncle Max has instructed so. I guess I don't have full information about it my dear," Michelle lied. She knew it was bad to do so to the little princes but all the same, she needed not to know about the great surprise ahead of her.

"I guess I can tell what uncle Max is up to!" Sophie said her eyes glowing delightedly. Michelle turned to her puzzled.

"Are you sure?" she asked and the little girl nodded.

"Alright, go on and tell your aunt all about it then," Michelle said in a childish voice leaving Sophie in great laughter.

"I think it is for a birthday party or Christmas!" the girl answered boldly.

"Why do you think so?" Michelle asked amid laughter.

"Every time one of us has a birthday, mother ensures that she fills the house with all kinds of decorations. She does the same during the Christmas too," Sophie answered smiling winsomely.

"That's brilliant!" Michelle said applauding, "You are a very intelligent girl. What do you want to become when you grow up?"

"I would like to join the military!" she said joyfully.

"The military; are you serious?" Michelle asked puzzled while abandoning what she was doing at the moment.

"Yes aunt, uncle Max is in the military too. He saved my life and I want to save people's lives too," Sophie answered twisting her head in pleasure.

"That sounds interesting. Did uncle Max tell you that he is in the military?"

"No, I heard him telling the doctors the day he took me to the big hospital that, he is an ex-military Captain."

"He said that he is an ex-military Captain?'' Michelle couldn't believe her ears.

Sophie must have heard everything wrong. Max was still in the military. How could he have left without her knowledge? She remembered very well that, the last time she paid him a visit is on receiving the news of his hospitalization after that head injury during one of his missions. She came to check on him when he was admitted to the hospital and he never told her anything about resigning or losing his job.

Neither did he tell her about it during their numerous conversations over the phone for the past months. All she knew was that whenever she paid him a visit, he always asked for a leave until her visit was over. Therefore, she thought that he had done the same even for now.

They went on chatting on various things until they completed their decorating work. However, Michelle chose not to ignore Sophie's information and she decided to ask Max all about it. All the same, she was to find a suitable moment to do that; after Miss Hassan's welcoming party.

* * *

The Girl From America

The following day in the afternoon, Max and the three teachers set out to Kikuyu General Hospital to pick Miss Hassan. Max had told the doctor about the party and had agreed to officially discharge her exactly at the time they would go to pick her.

Michelle, Sophie and other invited guests remained in the house and waited. Among them were Steve and Mark. The whole place appeared lively and heavenly. Steve, who knew all that had happened, was overwhelmed. Truly, Max and Michelle were decent people. He liked everything they were doing to Miss Hassan and her daughter. He desired a chance to talk to Miss Hassan as soon as she arrived and hear part of her story.

'If only she can allow us to publish the story in our news paper or magazine, I would be the happiest person under the Sun,' he thought going for another drink.

For the meantime, Michelle ensured that the guests could access all the services they needed. She also engaged in heated debates about life here in Kenya and America. Everyone present liked and admired how she handled everything.

'Max must be the happiest man to have such a beautiful intelligent woman with her.' Everyone thought.

In about an hour's time, their discussions and laughter were checkmated by the hooting sound of the car. They knew that it was Max announcing his arrival and everyone got set to meet Miss Hassan. Up to the moment, little Sophie had no hint of what was all the merry making about. She just moved around the living room playing with everyone joyfully. Everyone had seemed to like her as well.

"It's time!" Michelle announced as soon as the main door bell rung. They all stood up and got ready. As soon as Michelle opened the door, Max led Miss Hassan into the living room and the applauding and shouts of joy began. Miss Hassan could not believe her eyes.

"This is too much for me!" she said amid tears of joy. Her daughter ran to meet her. The mother and daughter hugged and shed tears of joy.

"I never knew they were doing it for you mom!" Sophie shouted and everyone broke in laughter.

"They are great Sophie. I don't know how I can thank them," Miss Hassan answered kissing her daughters cheeks.

As for Max and Michelle, there was no time to narrate stories of the past. For them, it was time to celebrate. Every second that passed was precious to them. They served the drinks and

after ensuring that everyone had a full glass, they made a hilarious toast. Afterwards, they went to the dining room and had a great nosh up. After that, they all suggested walking around Max's flower garden for some fresh air. More drinks were served and everyone walked around with a glass of champagne in their hands. Here, only Sophie constituted an exception. However, she had a glass of Delmonte mango juice; it was her favourite.

"It's great to meet you, Miss Hassan," Steve began the conversation as soon as he got close to her. There was no need for introductions between them because Max had already done that for everyone on their arrival.

"It's nice to meet you too!" Miss Hassan said while shaking hands once more.

"Forgive me Miss Hassan but I found your story quite interesting. I'm glad that you made it so quick. Congrats, " Steve said smoothly.

"Thank you Steve. But why do you find my story interesting?" Miss Hassan asked her eyes wide open.

"You see," Steve began, "I think with your permission I can get it prepared from the beginning to the end and air it on our T.V."

"Steve," Miss Hassan called after a sigh of relief, "I can't deny you the chance being one of Max's best friend. However, I must say you media

people know how to do your work perfectly. Believe it not, I had seen it coming as soon as Max introduced me to you," Miss Hassan said and both broke into laughter. Everyone at the garden turned on their direction.

"I think those two are getting along well," Max said to Michelle.

"How easily do you forget that Steve is a media person? He is just up to some business," Michelle replied in laughter.

"You might be right," Max said.

For the meantime, Sophie sat in the living room, in her hands was Max's phone playing a game that he had recently downloaded for her. The little girl enjoyed the game in peace knowing that her mother was well. She had wept bitterly at the hospital, when Max and Michelle took her there to see her mother. Everyone that day was in a sad mood including the doctors and they pitied her.

From that day, they agreed not to take her there again until. However, being in the company of her newly found uncle and aunt, she recovered before she went to bed that night. At the garden, Steve and miss Hassan decided to tell Max about it because he was the major character in the upcoming story.

"Steve, I think whatever I did was out of good will and I would not like to see the story

repeated on T.V or in your papers," Max said firmly.

"I understand Max. But Miss Hassan is okay with it and remember, she was one of the major victims of the dangerous riot," Steve said.
"I can clearly understand that but am not sure whether I like your ideas," Max said.

"It's alright darling," Michelle stated, "I understand everything you have done to them; you would wish it to remain within this circle but on the other hand, I think Steve is right. The story will be a big lesson to many citizens of this country. They will learn the virtue of doing good to others. Remember you told me that your greatest mission under the sun will be: doing well always. Let other people learn from this humble thing you have done. It might trigger many hearts and build a desire for them to follow your mission." Everyone among the four nodded.

"It's okay darling. I had not thought of it in that point of view. Thank you for making me see it in the right way," Max said and kissed her. Miss Hassan and Steve felt like doing the same. Later, they planned on how to start the story and everything was left to Steve and his media team.

* * *

All the guests left at 10.30pm. However, everything had turned out vivacious for everyone. Miss Hassan had a great time talking to his newly found brother and sister. She had never encountered someone she could call a brother or a sister in her life. She was born in the streets and raised in a children's home.

That's where she got full support in her education and everything else that she needed in course of her studies, and she left the children's home after completing her teaching course at the University of Nairobi, and was lucky enough to get a teaching job at a boarding school but later resigned and joined Ruiru Star Academy.

It's during her previous school where she met a Science male teacher and got married within a short period of courtship. However, as soon as she had given birth to her daughter, the husband abandoned her and eloped with another woman. She later learnt that he stayed in coastal province of the country. Since then, she made a decision to work hard for her daughter recalling the problems she had encountered since she was a young child.

Nonetheless, since that time, she had never been so cheerful again. She always considered the children's home as her only home but as per now; she had discovered the real happiness. She could now afford to call someone

a brother and another a sister. She thanked Max and Michelle a million times for their generosity, hospitality and wonderful love to her and her daughter. She was excited to learn that Michelle came from America and she disclosed her long desire to visit USA.

"I will plan that for you my dear sister. I'm very happy to find such a great friend too," Michelle told her. They talked until late in the night. By then, the little Sophie was sound asleep in her small room. Her mother was shown to her room, the one Michelle had occupied before and after checking on her daughter; she wished them a good night and went to sleep.

Max and Michelle remained in the living room in silence. He knew that there was only one bedroom left and he also knew very well that Michelle would disagree with him if he opted to spend the night on the couch. He watched his girlfriend who appeared deep in thoughts and smiled. Michelle felt the gravity of that smile and turned to him smiling too.

"Come on dear, I am feeling sleepy. I think we should go to sleep as well," Michelle said standing up. Max stood up and prepared himself for what was coming. After all, Michelle was his girlfriend for the last five years. He should not be afraid of her.

"I now remember I have a surprise for you," he broke out as soon as they reached his bedroom door.

"Come on dear. I'm so tired, can't it wait till tomorrow?" Michelle asked.

"It can't. Wait a minute," Max said rushing back to the living room. He checked in the cupboard drawers and picked a CD by Celine Dion. He had bought it the previous day and had not found a suitable moment to ask Michelle to listen to it. On getting back, he was shocked to find Michelle standing at the door of the bedroom waiting for him.

"Oh dear, you should have gone in."

"No, I opted to wait for you. Therefore, I will walk in after you," she said smiling.

"Alright," Max said pushing the door open. He went straight to the record player on one side of the room and switched it on. Michelle stood in the middle of the large room looking from one point to another.

'It is a great place he has here,' she always thought like this whenever she got in this room. Max glanced at her and smiled.

"Don't worry about the room. I made it so because of the kids. I will be playing basketball with them right in here," Max said still working on the record player. Michelle broke into

laughter and walked to the couch set near the bed.

The room seemed to have everything. Two couches, a fridge on one corner, a big study table with a computers on it, a six by six bed, two large wardrobes, a record player and a thirty two inches slim screen TV, a coffee table and a bookshelf on the wall.

'It's unbelievable. This is too much for a bedroom,' she thought again. She looked at him and smiled- Max was that entire she needed. She liked his deep voice and his gentle smile that drew everyone to him. She gazed at the baldness above his left ear where a bullet had whizzed past, and then contemplated on his muscular body and the strength of his bull neck shown in the twining cords of muscle that shaped his symmetrical body. Max had already inserted the CD in the disc player. He smiled and went to her. He bent and kissed her brow.

"The surprise will be up within a minute. What will you take?" he asked pointing at the fully packed fridge.

"Anything," she answered.

"You said anything? Wait a minute," he said picking two empty glasses from a tray on the coffee table.

"Oh my God, you got me red handed Max!" Michelle exclaimed jumping on her feet,

"Celine Dion is my favourite artist and the song too: 'BECAUSE YOU LOVED ME', you are incredible Max!'' she said in amusement.

"I always know what is good for you darling,'' Max said opening a bottle of champagne. He poured it in the two glasses and handed one to her. As they toasted their drinks in joy, she was in inestimable bliss.

"You've amazed me darling,'' she said. As they sipped their drinks, the song was already halfway. They kept silent in order to listen and enjoy and mull over its notes.

"Would you mind a dance?'' he asked.

"Dancing is always in me, I used to dance a lot when I was a kid,'' she answered. Max placed the empty glasses on the table and held her by her waist. They began making smooth moves as per the rhythm of the song.

"Thank you for everything darling, you are my best!'' she said.

"No dear. *I want to be your favourite and forget the rest!*'' he stated and they broke in laughter.

"You are a darling,'' she said and they kissed.

Max moved her slowly towards the record player. The music was now over but they still remained in the same dancing motion. He stretched his hand and switched it off still holding

her by his right hand. He then walked to the electric switch and as he was about to place his finger on it, Michelle pulled him away.

"Are you afraid of the lights?" she asked.

"During my military missions, I always waited until it was night so that I could attack my enemies better," he replied boldly.

"Alright, but in our case, there is no enemies and therefore the lights must be on," she said in laughter and walked towards the study table. She lit the large glass lantern. Max switched off the lights and the lantern's light sparkled in the room.

"You are a genius!" Max said holding her in his arms.

"I suppose the military captain is now prepared for the battle!" she said and they broke in laughter. In no time, they were kissing and plummeting on the bed.

* * *

The following day, everyone in the house woke up late. After the breakfast, Max and Michelle were ready to escort Miss Hassan and her daughter to their place. On getting there, the neighbours were pleased to see Miss Hassan and her daughter again. Max and Michelle found themselves in another celebratory moment.

After ensuring that everything was in order, they left promising to pay them visits as much as they could and vice versa. Sophie was a little troubled to part with them, but she was told that they would be checking on them frequently. They also assured her that they would be spending the weekend together. Max and Michelle drove back to their place.

CHAPTER 6

It was the third month since Michelle arrived in the country. Her reason for the visit was one-Max. Her visit was good and she enjoyed it more than any other before. Max had told her that they would be visiting his parents place, at the slopes of Mt. Kenya. She had never seen the mountain and only read about it in the internet or and sometimes in a journal called, Encounters of Africa. Now, another great thing was on the way, she would see it for real.

On the other hand, Max had set everything in order to ensure that his girl would attach importance to the visit. He had called his parents to announce their visit. He had kept telling them about the American girl he had fallen in love with but were not sure whether their son's brain was functioning properly.

"I think the sounds of guns had driven him crazy," his father said to his mother the evening Max called to announce their visit.

"You can't speak like that of our son. I know Max very well and I can't wait to meet the girl," His mother always defended him.

"Then why has he not brought her around for all those years? You keep waiting but at the same time prepare for a heart attack if his story turns out to be a joke," he warned.

"For all the people I know, I will be the last Max can deceive," she said and left the living room. She remembered how hard she kept praying for Max to marry soon. He was already thirty and she feared he might grow too old without a wife.

Her husband remained in the living room reading his favourite-Riverwood Magazine. Max ensured that he sent one to him every week.

"The children of today have really changed. I wonder when his mother will realize that," he said and went on turning the pages until his eyes landed on Max's photo in company of two women and a kid. He quickly read through the headline of the story, 'An ex-military Captain becomes a Captain of Good Deeds'. He then scrutinized through the photos and reread the headline again.

"What has he done this time? It doesn't look like another bullet in the head," he said in a small voice. He then decided to read the story first before mentioning a thing about it to his wife. From a far, you could see that he was enjoying the read. His eyes brightened and he kept balancing his reading glasses well above his nose now and then in pleasure. At last he placed the magazine on the table and smiled.

"I'm happy to see that my son has done such a great thing," he nodded his head in joy

and now remembered he should call his wife. In a few minutes, his wife was at the story. She began dancing even before she was through. The husband rested and waited. In no time, she was through.

"I told you Max is a great boy. He can't lie to us. They have already mentioned about his girlfriend from America," she said excited, "she looks beautiful too!" she added hysterically. At this point, Max's father could not believe his ears. His wife must be adding her things on the content. He snatched the magazine from her hands and quickly read through the story. In no time, he couldn't believe his eyes; he had skipped the line that mentioned about Max's girlfriend: Michelle Catalane. Now he realized that his son was no longer a joker as he had thought.

"He has chosen well, isn't it?" his wife asked in bliss.

"I bet I hadn't seen this sentence," he said pointing at the context, "As per my thinking, she looks great," he said. His wife bent and kissed his forehead.

"I'm glad to hear that from the big boy. I'm also glad to see our son did a marvelous job by saving a young life. Now, I must get back to preparations before your daughter gets back from town," she said walking out of the room.

"Don't expect them so soon. I know they

must spend time there telling their friends about Max and his girlfriend's visit tomorrow," he assured his wife.

"Yeah, I know this house will be fully packed like a stadium tomorrow," she said going back to the kitchen.

"I got such a funny wife and son. I think I'm blessed," he said turning another page of the magazine. Then, he remembered that he should call and thank him for his good work.

* * *

Early the following morning, Max's jeep roared making its way towards the slopes of Mt. Kenya. Michelle was beyond herself with joy because she was to meet Max's parents and his two sisters. She remembered how she longed to see them when Max told her about them and how glad she was when Max sent their photos to her a year ago. Max told her that her sisters were long married but assured her that they would be present with their kids and husbands.

"You must be having great nieces and nephews," she had told him at the time. For the moment, she concentrated on taking photos and short videos along the way. Max liked to see her in such happiness.

He secretly knew that she was heading to the climax of her joy. She would soon meet his people. They arrived in the town after a three hour drive. Max drove to a petrol station to refill his jeep and Michelle rushed for soft drinks at the nearest shop. In a few minutes, they were back to the jeep and driving towards Max's place.

"The town you saw is the centre of commerce in this county," Max stated.

"It appears great. I like it," she said.

"When I was in high school, it was just a little town with a few tall buildings. That time everything was under the national government. But after the coming of the devolution government, the governor has overseen its development to where it is now within a period of three years. Since then, it has attracted numerous investors and that's why you have seen colleges, universities, financial institutions and many other kinds of investments almost in every corner of it."

"Then you should be thankful to the devolved government," Michelle said smiling.

"That's true. My dear, we are now one kilometer away. How do you feel about the journey?" he asked.

"It's really awesome. I feel like those times when I used to drive madly from New York to Texas!" she answered in laughter. "Are you

serious? Though I have never been to that place I used to read about it in the internet. It's comparatively far!'' Max exclaimed.

"You are right. But then I enjoyed driving. I had just bought a new car and I remembered most of the weekends, I spent the time on the road.''

"If it were not for the photographing and the like, I could have asked you to drive,'' Max said.

"Don't mind about that. I promise to do it on our way back,'' she said joyfully.

"But not until six days are over!'' Max announced.

"You don't have to worry about that darling. I wish I could spend a life time here. But my leave is almost done. I don't want to think about it either.''

"It's alright. I believe our time here will be the most enjoyable and cherished moment ever. I promise to do everything within my power to achieve that.''

"I greatly appreciate you dear,'' she said.

"You are welcome,'' he added smiling winsomely.

Max slowed down and turned his jeep to his right, they had already arrived. They glanced at each other and smiled. The place was packed with people and Max seemed to recognize some

of his old friends.

Majority of his friends had heard about the American girl and couldn't miss such a golden chance to meet her. As Max drove towards his father's parking, he could tell that it was a great moment for them.

Michelle was overwhelmed with joy too. His mother was the first to meet them; she hugged him joyfully and went for Michelle. She hugged her and began dancing in joy. Max's sisters came second, then the owner of the house who was watching from a distance followed and then everyone else. Max did his best to introduce his friends to Michelle and other relatives present.

"It's a beauty you have here. This is too much for a soldier!" One of his former schoolmates teased leaving everyone in laughter. Max and Michelle had known what would befall them and they had shopped enough for everyone. No one present missed a gift. It was an animating moment for everyone.   His mother was the happiest. She couldn't let her eyes go off Michelle for a second.

"They should know I need a grandchild soon. Whether it will be born in America or right here in Kenya I won't mind," she whispered.

* * *

Days were moving so fast, Max thought. They were already counting their fourth day in the village. There was a lot for Michelle to see and learn. They travelled to other villages, tea and coffee farms, fish ponds and she could not believe the adventurous she was in. She liked how people handled their daily routines from farming to business.

"How I wish you had brought me here the day of my arrival. I can't believe I have been missing all this for the last five years. That's not fair Max," Michelle complained that evening. They were in Max's house. The building looked similar to the one in the city but was not fully equipped as the same.

"It seems you had the same idea of setting up another basketball pitch here," Michelle said to Max looking around the bedroom.

"You are right;" Max had answered in laughter.

"Then you will make the best father ever!" she stated.

"That has been my dream since I was a little kid. You will too make the best mother ever, I can bet on that," Max said. A silence followed. Michelle walked about the room and at last sat on the bed.

"I think we have hiked a lot today, you

must be very tired," Max said.

"You are right but I feel okay. I loved the hiking too," she replied.

"We have only two days left. So tomorrow I will be taking you to the foot of Mt. Kenya. I guess it will be too cold for you." At the mention of this, Michelle brightened. She knew that another great adventure awaited her. Although they could clearly see the mountain from Max's place, she knew it would look even better standing somewhere below it.

"Thank you so much dear. I knew from the start that I fell in love with the right person. Someone who knows exactly what it's like to be in love," she said kissing him.

"Thank you darling. My desire is to make you the happiest woman in this planet," he said as they both sat on the bed.

At this point, Michelle realized that it was time to ask that important question. She had tried her best to find the right moment and then she knew it was time. "Max," she called calmly, "Are you still in the military?" she asked. Max immediately rose up. He knew he had messed up by not telling her all about it since she arrived in the country, even after being so opportunistic about it.

"I'm so sorry dear," he said turning to face her, "I beg you to forgive me. You see, many

things have happened since your arrival and I kept thinking that I had already told you about it," he paused and a silence followed.

"The truth is, I left military three months later after recovering from the head injury. At the time you had already gone back. I know you might wonder why I didn't tell you over the phone during our many calls but, I thought it would be better if I waited and explain it one on one," he said sitting beside her once more.

"It's alright. What prompted you to quit?" she asked. Then he narrated all the happenings and how everyone advised him to do it for his own wellbeing.

"I understand darling. I regret all that happened without my knowledge. But I am happy I have you, strong, hale and hearty," she said embracing him warmly.

"Thank you so much," Max said.

"So what have you planned to do now that you have no job" she asked in a serious tone than Max expected. He hesitated and then laughed a little; he then composed himself and looked straight in her eyes.

"I know this will be a great surprise not only to you but to my family as well. They know I hated books so much during my school time," he said and Michelle looked at him surprised.

"So, are you planning to resume your studies?" she asked.

"The truth is that I had done further studies when I was still in the military. What I mean here is that, I have decided to become a writer!" he stated.

"What? I can't believe my ears. So what kind of writing will you engage yourself to?" she asked puzzled.

"Creative writing," he answered.

Michelle was wordless for a moment. She loved books and more so, novels and short stories. Now that her boyfriend will be a writer, she would be the happiest woman and a great fan of his work.

"Have you begun the writing?" she asked.

"Yes. My first manuscript is already in the hands of the publishers. It's a great read."

"Will you mind telling me what the book entails?"

"Mmmh... for now all you need to know is that it's a good story," Max said.

"Come on darling, I can't handle my anticipation anymore. May I know the title of the book?" she asked soothingly.

"It's all right because I know you will not take no for an answer. The book is titled," he paused and looked at her. Michelle waited anxiously.

"The Girl from America!" he announced. Michelle jumped from the bed. She then turned to Max bewildered. Max stood before her.

"It's your story my dear. I want the world to read about you. The present and the future generation!" he declared.

"I don't know what I will do to you. I must do something to you!" she screamed joyfully pulling his ears, "this is too much for me soldier!" By then, Max was amid great laughter. He never knew she would turn so hysterical.

"You can do whatever you wish my dear. I'm all yours, split my ears if that's all what you want!" he stated still in laughter. She kissed him dearly.

* * *

The visit to Mt. Kenya ended up very successful. Michelle confessed it was as cold as winter in America. However, she had a story to tell her people. She knew that they would not rest until they also paid it a visit. She took as many photos as her camera could manage. While there, Max searched for one of the highest rocks and after climbing on it, he loudly announced that he was in love with Michelle. His voice thundered and echoed through the rocks and forest.

"You are mad!" Michelle shouted in laughter.

"Yes. I am madly in love with you. Will you be my wife?" Max shouted from the same point. Michelle run and climbed on another rock next to him.

"Yes Max!" she shouted, "I will be your wife!"

They climbed down and sealed their engagement with a kiss. That evening, they went back home in bliss, side by side like flora and fauna. However, whenever Michelle looked at the diamond ring that Max had given to her while at the mountain; she felt greatly joyful than ever before.

They left the village the following morning amid great joy. Max's parents wished them well and a safe journey. Her sisters had also arrived early enough to bid them farewell including his relatives and closest friends.

* * *

Back in Nairobi, they rested for a while and started setting up everything for Michelle's departure. Her leave was over and she would be flying back to America the following day.

"Max, I want you to take me to the hospital," Michelle said late in the evening. Max was aghast. He thought that Michelle was ill.

"Is everything okay?" he asked.

"Yes, I dearly need a medical checkup. It's

important,'' she replied.

Max never insisted for an explanation. He was ready to do anything and everything for her. They drove to the National Hospital and in less than an hour, they were already there. Max didn't worry too much because Michelle was a doctor herself and she knew exactly what to do. However, on their way to the hospital, Max had kept enquiring whether she was fine and she assured him that all was well with her. He remained aghast. On arrival, she asked him to wait at the reception hall and he sat there for not less than twenty minutes when a nurse came for him.

He was still stunned but after enquiring, the nurse assured him that all was well. They went to the office adjacent to the medical examination room. He found Michelle seated in a company of one doctor and two nurses chatting hilariously. On getting inside, the doctor and his team left and went in another room.

"Take a seat dear,'' Michelle said. Without wasting time, she handed him the medical examination report. Max swiftly began checking through it.

"What! I can't believe this. What a wonderful surprise. This is great news!'' he shouted looking up at Michelle, "I love children honey. I can't believe I will be a father!'' Max

went on shouting hysterically. Michelle smiled amid tears of joy. They hugged and kissed in elation.

"You should have told me about it at first!" Max complained.

"I wanted to be a hundred percent sure before telling you about it," Michelle answered.

The doctor and his team joined them. They wished them well and they left. That evening, they paid a visit at Miss Hassan's place and Michelle bid them goodbye. They had already informed Miss Hassan about her departure earlier. They also paid a visit to some of Max's friends including Steve and Captain Mark, who wished her a safe flight.

In the following day, the two of them were already in the airport at 9.00am. Michelle's flight was scheduled at 9.30am. It was a cheerful parting moment because they knew very well that, they would meet soon.

"I will dearly wait for that book darling," she said. Max took his mobile phone and called the publishers. He enquired on the proceedings and he was assured that the book would be out in the next three weeks. After the conversation, he told Michelle about it.

"I wish I had a little more time left," she said.

"Don't worry, I promise to send it to you

as soon as I get the copies, '' Max assured her. They hugged and remained in that state for some minutes. Then they heard a voice via a megaphone announcing that the plane would set off to America by the next ten minutes.

"For how long will I be expecting you?'' Michelle asked.

"Two weeks after sending the book,'' he answered.

"I will have missed you to death," she said poking his nose. They headed to the plane. Most of the military security team at the airport knew Max and winked their eyes to him as he passed by with his girlfriend.

"I have something in mind dear?'' Max began saying, "I want us to set up two homes: one in Kenya and the other in America.''

"That's a brilliant idea. I do support you," she said. On getting near the plane, Max hugged and kissed her. He wished her a safe flight and she promised to get in touch as soon as she arrived.

"I know I will miss you darling,'' she said amid tears.

"I will miss you too!'' Max answered firmly.

He went back to the waiting bay and waited until the plane left. He then took his jeep and drove back to his place. Even though he felt

lonely, he knew that they would be together soon. He poured some wine in a glass and sipped relaxing on the couch.

"I know she will like the book," he thought aloud. He sipped his drink slowly to the end. He turned on the TV and in a few minutes, he was snoring.

THE END